MEGA
MA

MW00998124

BIG
TRUCKS

Super Explorers

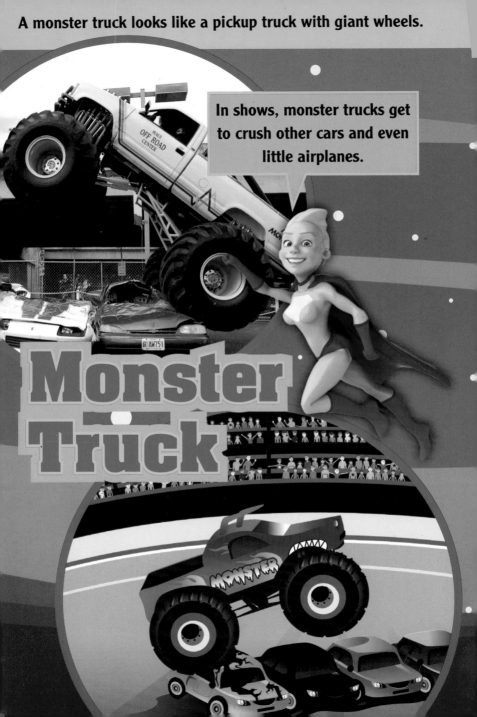

A monster truck looks like a pickup truck with giant wheels.

In shows, monster trucks get to crush other cars and even little airplanes.

Monster Truck

You can only see these trucks in special shows. They can't drive on roads like normal trucks. The trucks do tricks. Sometimes they spin around or stand on their back wheels. They even do jumps.

The giant tires are almost as tall as a grownup. They let the truck drive over almost anything.

A monster truck has a stronger body than a pickup truck. The truck can roll over but the driver will be safe.

Monster truck engines are very powerful. They use a special kind of fuel. Monster truck shows are fun to watch but they are very loud. People at the show have to wear earplugs.

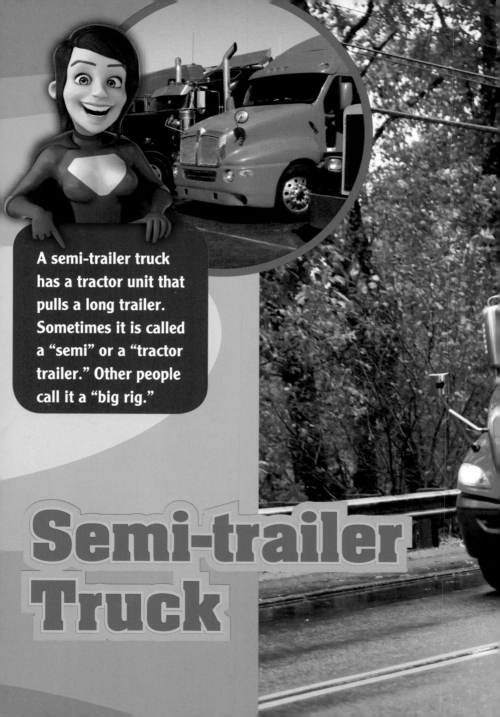

A semi-trailer truck has a tractor unit that pulls a long trailer. Sometimes it is called a "semi" or a "tractor trailer." Other people call it a "big rig."

Semi-trailer Truck

The tractor unit has a cab where the driver sits. Behind the cab is a sleeper where the driver can sleep at night on long trips.

A fire engine is a special kind of truck designed for fighting fires. It takes firefighters to the fire, pumps water and carries equipment for firefighting and rescue.

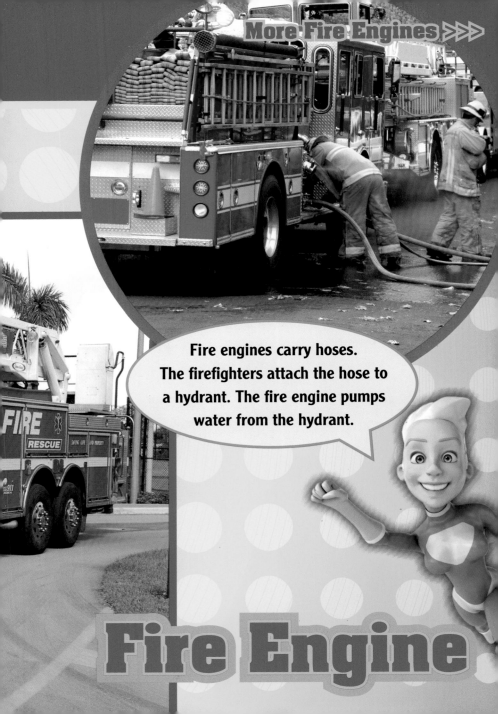

Fire engines carry hoses. The firefighters attach the hose to a hydrant. The fire engine pumps water from the hydrant.

Fire Engine

A fire engine can carry up to eight firefighters. Each firefighter has a special job so when they get to the fire, they can go to work right away.

Some garbage trucks pick up large containers called dumpsters. The truck has special forks that pick up the dumpster and lift it up to empty it.

Other trucks open at the back or the side so that waste collectors can empty bins into them.

Garbage Truck

Garbage trucks collect trash from homes and businesses. They take it to a waste management site or landfill.

More Garbage Trucks >>>

Concrete mixers have large drums that hold wet concrete. A spiral blade in the drum turns and mixes the concrete. It keeps the concrete from getting hard.

When the truck reaches the construction site, the drum tips down. The concrete comes out of the drum and goes down a chute.

Concrete mixers are also called "cement trucks" or "cement mixers."

Concrete Mixer

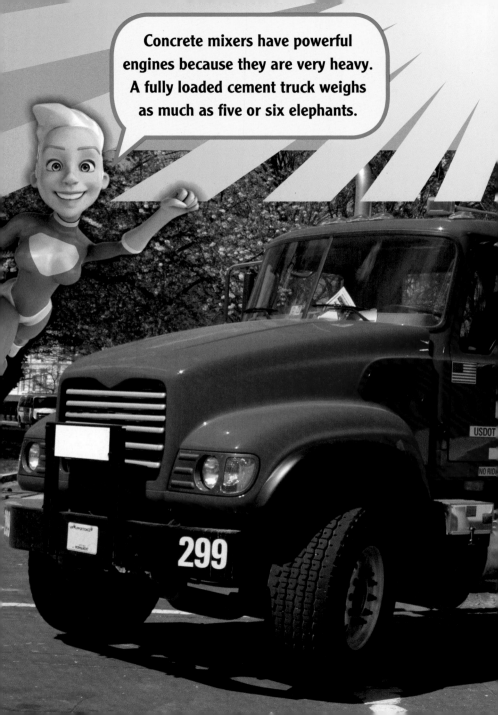

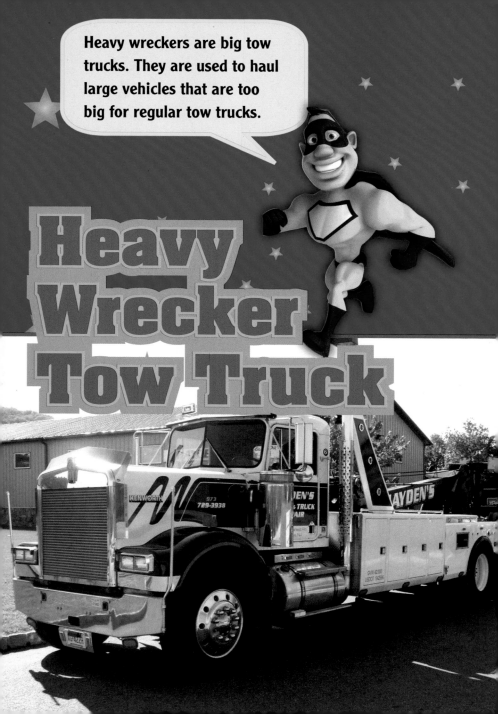

Sometimes a large truck tips over on its side. The heavy wrecker can use its crane to pull the truck upright again.

Heavy wreckers can tow buses and semi-trailer trucks. They can even pull concrete mixers. Some heavy wreckers have flatbeds to carry cars, trucks or equipment.

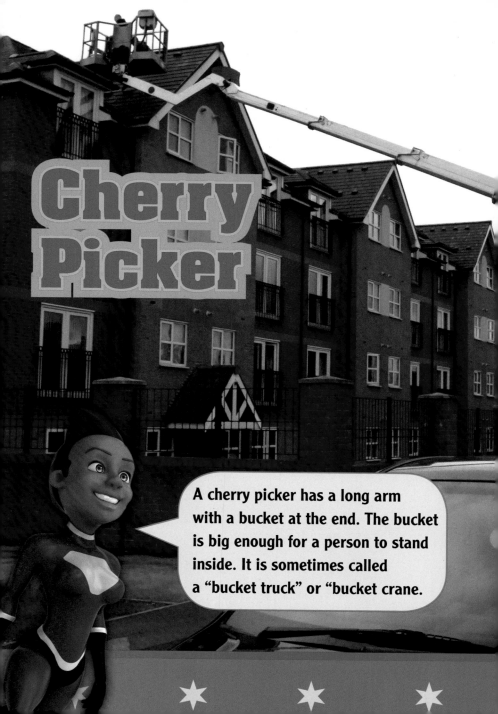

Cherry Picker

A cherry picker has a long arm with a bucket at the end. The bucket is big enough for a person to stand inside. It is sometimes called a "bucket truck" or "bucket crane."

The person in the bucket has controls to move the arm up and down. There are also controls at the base of the arm.

Street Sweeper

Street sweepers clean our roads. They remove gravel and garbage from our streets. Many cities use street sweepers to clean the roads in spring after the snow melts.

These trucks are used to clean big storage tanks and oil spills. They also clear away mud from drilling rigs.

Vacuum Truck

Vacuum trucks usually empty their tanks at a wastewater treatment plant.

These trucks drive on gravel roads in the forest and on paved highways.

Logging trucks must have powerful motors because the logs are very heavy. They usually travel slowly.

Logging Truck

Special stackers load and unload the logging truck.

Snowplows have big blades at the front. The blade scrapes up the snow and pushes it to the side.

Snowplows are usually yellow. They have many flashing lights so that car drivers can see them.

Snowplows have winter tires or special tires with studs so that they don't get stuck in the snow.

Sanding trucks put sand and salt on roads. The sand and salt mixture is called "grit." The grit helps melt the snow and ice so that people can drive safely.

Sanding Truck

Some people call sanding trucks "salt shakers."

The Unimog is a German truck. It was originally a farm truck but now it is used in other ways.

The Unimog has large wheels, and the body of the truck is high off the ground. That means it can drive almost anywhere. You can find Unimogs in mountains, jungles and deserts.

Unimog means "Universal Motor Gerät." "Gerät" is a German word that means "machine."

Many different countries use the Unimog. You can find it almost anywhere in the world.

Most cars and trucks have the steering wheel on the left side. The steering wheel of a Unimog can be on the right side or on the left side.

A Unimog can climb steep hills. It can also go in water that is more than a metre (3 feet) deep. It can climb over rocks that are a metre high.

Armies sometimes use amphibious trucks. The trucks have thick armour to protect them during a war.

Dump trucks usually carry sand, dirt or gravel. In winter, they sometimes carry snow.

Dump Truck

These trucks usually work at construction sites. They take away loads of dirt. Sometimes they deliver sand or gravel to a construction site.

The tires of a haul truck are 4 metres (13 feet) high. That's higher than two people standing one on top of the other.

Haul Truck

World's Biggest Truck

The biggest truck in the world is the Belaz 75710. It's as long as two buses parked end to end. It weighs more than a fully loaded jumbo jet.

This truck has 8 tires—4 at the back and 4 at the front. Each giant tire has enough rubber to make 600 regular car tires.

Terex 6300AC

401

401

More of the World's Biggest Trucks

LIEBHERR

T 282 C

T 282 C

Liebherr T 282 C

Caterpillar 797F

Hitachi
EH5000AC-3

Komatsu
960E

The Publisher: Mega Machines is an imprint of Blue Bike Books

Library and Archives Canada Cataloguing in Publication

Big trucks / Super Heroes.
(Mega machines)
Issued in print and electronic formats.

ISBN 978-1-926700-64-9 (paperback).
ISBN 978-1-926700-66-3 (pdf)

1. Trucks—Juvenile literature. I. Super Heroes (Children's author), author

TL230.15.B53 2016   j629.224   C2016-901105-4
                                             C2016-901106-2

Front cover credits: Haul truck, Maksym Dragunov/Thinkstock; super heroes, julos/Thinkstock.

Back cover credits : Fire truck, JohnnyH5/Thinkstock; snowplow, otispug/Thinkstock; monster truck, USAF Sr Airman Larry E Reid Jr/Wikipedia.

Photo Credits: Every effort has been made to accurately credit the sources of photographs and illustrations. Any errors or omissions should be reported directly to the publisher for correction in future editions. *From Comstock Images:* Comstock Images, 58. *From Flickr:* mandolin, 2; John Wright, 3; laboiteverte, 42; OR Dept of Transport, 42; Brian Fagan, 44; Surrey county Council, 45; Rocky Chrysler, 46; LoadedAaron, 47; hmboo, 48; yetdark, 48. *From Thinkstock:* illus_artistico, 2; cosmonaut, 9; DanielMirer, 6; Pixelci, 9; vitpho, 6-7; CHUYN, 13; egdigital, 11; JiriNovotny, 12; JohnnyH5, 15; kadmy, 17; Laura Eisenberg, 17; Paul Vasarhelyi, 16; Roman Klimov, 14; aguirre_mar, 18; Albert Cheng, 21; Anton Foltin, 18; jim pruitt, 19, 20; Jim Parkin, 28; leah613, 29; Steven Frame, 27; Arthur Preston, 31; beloitwi, 31; Kuzma, 30; Darin Burt, 34; MakaronProduktion, 35; mariakraynova, 38; tfoxfoto, 40; Craig Uglinica, 41; Robert Pernell, 56; Roman Milert, 57; sewer11, 54; Tracy Fox, 56; Tracy Fox, 55; bondgrunge, 59; belaz75710, 61; belaz75710, 60; directindustry, 63; exzellent, 63; C_carinpicture, 62. *From Wikipedia:* Tammy Powers, 4; USAF Sr Airman Larry E Reid Jr, 4; Thomas Schoch, 8-9; Wankach, 10; Mfield, 12-13; Antti Leppanen, 22, 37; Steve Pivnick_USAF, 23; Ingolfson, 23; Cts1033, 25; Anthony Appleyard, 26-27; Vac-Con_, 32; Skraldesuger, 33; Benchill, 36; Jeroen Kransen, 38-39; UnreifeKirsche, 40; katy, 43; Klaus Nahr, 46; Harald Hansen, 50; Zandcee, 51; Kiril Kapustin, 52; Thomas Love, 52; TCSGT, 59; Jay 1327, 62; Autografia Hungary, 63.

Background Graphics: IgorZakowski/Thinkstock, 2, 3, 6, 23, 35, 38, 58, 63; shelma1/Thinkstock, 4, 21, 40, 44, 55; NoraVector/Thinkstock, 10, 41, 45; Lana_Stem/Thinkstock, 13, 53, 56; kennykiernan/Thinkstock, 15, 43; Daniel Rodriguez Quintana/Thinkstock, 18, 26, 56; DavidGrigg/Thinkstock, 24, 28, 31, 46.

Superhero Illustrations: julos/Thinkstock.

Produced with the assistance of the Government of Alberta, Alberta Media Fund.

We acknowledge the financial support of the Government of Canada through the Canada Book Fund for our publishing activities.

Government

Funded by the Government of Canada
Financé par le gouvernement du Canada

PC: 35